MW00886848

Do the Sharks Have Shoes?

Carolyn Williams

ISBN 978-1-0980-4622-4 (paperback)
ISBN 978-1-0980-8052-5 (hardcover)
ISBN 978-1-0980-4623-1 (digital)

Christian Faith Publishing, Inc.
832 Park Avenue
Meadville, PA 16335
www.christianfaithpublishing.com

Printed in the United States of America

In memory of my mother, Carrie, my Guiding Light.

Dedicated with love to my son,
Christopher, daughter-in-law, Angela, and
grandchildren, Michaela and Jarrod.

I persevere at procrastination. Not a good thing. For the love of my family above, great satisfaction and joy I've had, with the help of others, in completing this book.

It was a most glorious September morning. As the warmth of the sun kissed the earth, the white clouds did a slow glide across the blue sky. Gazing at the heavens on this morn, with a little imagination, one might think the clouds were whispering, "This is your day. Be happy. Use it well."

Michelle, 11, and Daniel, nine, were off from school this day due to a water main break on their school's street. An ice-cream and pizza party couldn't have made the two of them happier. A few kids at the school, a very few, had their own name for unscheduled days off from school: Time Out of School Day–TOOSday.

Michelle and Daniel's parents took turns taking them to school. After having made breakfast with them, their father was taking them to their grandmother's house.

When they arrived, Michelle, nicknamed Mic Mic, and Daniel greeted their Grandmother Susie who simply wanted to be called Granny.

Susie's mother's name was Carrie. They called her Ms. Carrie instead of Great Granny. After greetings were made, hugs and kisses given, their father, Archie, left for work.

Susie started brushing her mother's hair.

With the TV on, Mic Mic and Daniel were watching the morning news shows. There was news about a bear attack and shark attacks. Michelle turned to Granny and said, "There has been a lot of news about shark attacks this summer."

Her Granny replied, "I know. I heard it has been called the summer of the sharks."

Daniel chimed in, "I sure don't want to go swimming at the beach."

To which Mic Mic replied, "Sharks are not at every beach. There're places you can swim where there aren't any sharks."

Daniels response was, "You go right ahead, Mic. I'll visit you in the hospital or morgue."

Granny chimed in, "Enough, Daniel. Say no more!"

Daniel knew by the tone of Granny's voice she was serious. Just a little angry, to say the least. Daniel said nothing more. He was kidding with his sister.

As Ms. Carrie looked at the TV. She had a blank look on her face. It was as if she didn't know what was going on. Ms. Carrie was diagnosed with dementia. In short, she had memory loss, lack of judgement and reasoning. She could no longer take care of herself. Activities of Daily Living, ADL, she could no longer perform. Ms. Carrie could no longer cook, which she loved to do.

At the beginning of her dementia, she gave then toddler, Daniel, the name Dubious Dan. As she watched him play one afternoon, he couldn't decide whether he wanted to build with his blocks, bounce his ball, or pull his wagon with his plush polar bear in it. Ms. Carrie shouted, "Daniel!"

He turned, looked at her, and smiled.

"You just don't know what to do, Dubious Dan."

He ran to her, arms open with the biggest grin on his face. He hugged her as best he could with his little arms. Because of his reaction, his family called him Dubious Dan for a little while. But as he grew, he was anything but doubtful or indecisive.

Michelle and Daniel could see changes in their great grandmother as they grew older. Ms. Carrie sometimes remembered Mic Mic and Daniel. More often, they were strangers to her. Today, she seemed to recognize them.

While the news continued, there was another mention of a shark attack. “Do the sharks have shoes?” Ms. Carrie asked.

Mic Mic and Daniel looked at her as if to ask, “Has she lost her mind?” Even knowing her condition, the question took them by surprise.

Michelle blurted out, “Ms. Carrie, sharks don’t have feet. They have fins and swim in oceans.”

Ms. Carrie turned to her daughter and said, “The sharks need shoes, just like you do. I want you to take my charge and buy them some shoes.”

Susie repeated what Mic Mic just said, “Sharks have fins, not feet, and they swim in the oceans.”

"So what? They need shoes!" Ms. Carrie exclaimed.

Susie learned a long time ago not to argue with her mother, knowing the damage to her brain caused by dementia. She went along with what she said. Susie asked her, "How many pairs of shoes do you want me to buy?"

"Buy all the sharks shoes," Ms. Carrie said as she burst out in laughter as if she knew what she was saying made no sense. With a smile on her face, she said, "I kept shoes on your feet. I'm going to keep shoes on the sharks' feet."

Susie smiled at her mother and said, "Okay, Mom, I'll buy the sharks shoes. We're going to the oceans so you can see the shoes you bought them. We'll have a lot of fun."

With a smile on her face, Ms. Carrie said, "Okay, girl."

"Sharks don't have feet, Ms. Carrie, they have fins!" Mic Mic shouted at Ms. Carrie as she tried to explain again why they do not need shoes.

Ms. Carrie laughed some more, smiled again, and said, "We're going to see them. You need to go."

Mic Mic mumbled to herself, "Ms. Carrie, you're crazy."

Ms. Carrie heard and understood she was just called crazy. In an angry voice, she said to Mic Mic, "Don't you ever call me crazy!"

"Listen, Michelle," Granny continued, "don't you ever mumble or speak that way to your Great Granny again. You apologize, now!"

Mic Mic stood up, went over to Ms. Carrie, and told her she was truly sorry for what she said and how she spoke to her. "I know I'm wrong. Please forgive me."

At that moment, Ms. Carrie had no response. As Mic Mic sat down, head in her hands, Ms. Carrie looked as if she understood every word Mic Mic said and, in a quiet, calm, and forgiving voice, spoke the words, "I love you, Mic."

As the news continued, there was breaking news about an airplane crashing into a building in New York City. It was identified as the North Tower of One World Trade center. Mic Mic, Daniel, and Granny watched in awe at the horrific scene as live pictures of white smoke, black smoke, and fire were being shown. Ms. Carrie had a blank stare on her face. It was being reported that it was definitely an airplane that had flown into the North Tower.

Mic Mic exclaimed, "How did that happen?"

Daniel blurted out, "That can't be an accident. It had to be done on purpose!"

To everyone's surprise, Ms. Carrie said, "They need a whooping! Their mothers need to whoop them for driving into the building. That's not nice. They bad." After a long pause, Ms. Carrie added, "They couldn't see where they were driving."

Daniel shook his head and told Ms. Carrie the airplane was flown in to the tower, not driven into it, and everyone on the plane was dead.

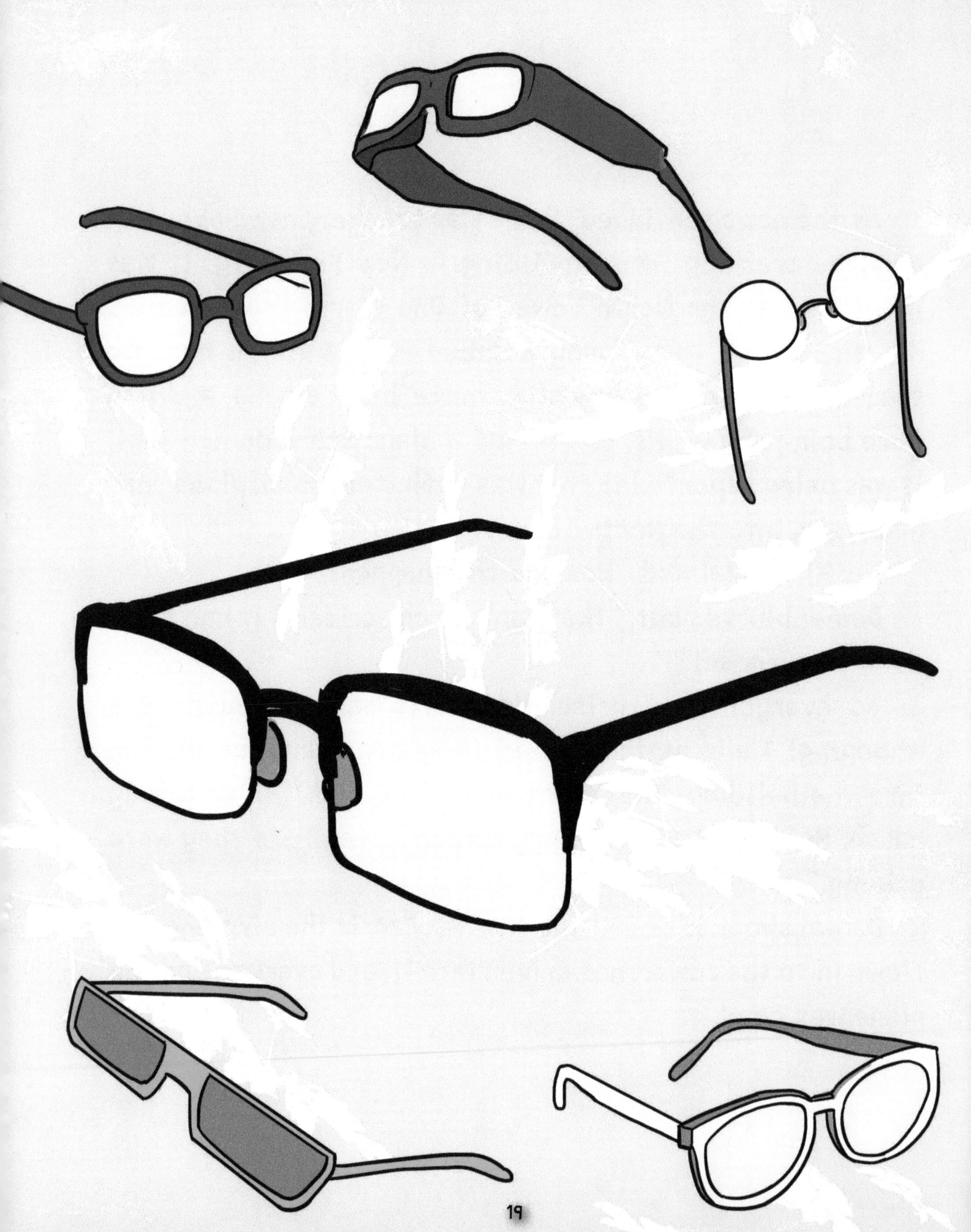

Ms. Carrie said, "They are not dead. They need glasses to where to drive next. Their mothers ought to be ashamed for not buying them eyeglasses."

Looking at Susie, Ms. Carrie said, "Take my charge and buy them glasses, so they can see where they are driving. You buy the shark shoes, and you buy them glasses so they can see where to drive next." Ms. Carrie smiled again. Did she know what she was saying? Was she playing with them?

Mic Mic got up to get a pen and paper in hand.

Sitting at the coffee table, she reflected on the things Ms. Carrie said. Seemingly to ponder on her spoken words, she wrote:

Shoes for the sharks swimming in the oceans so blue

Eyeglasses for the dead, Ms. Carrie hasn't a clue

Mic Mic showed Daniel what she had written. With those words written on paper, they confirmed what they already knew. They would never taste the best cornbread, drop buttermilk biscuits, or have the best parker house rolls in the world. They would never taste the best macaroni and cheese or fried chicken in the universe again.

As Michelle and Daniel looked at each other with sadness in their eyes, as their parents taught them, no matter how you feel-good, bad, happy, or sad-look up and say a little prayer. Michelle and Daniel talked to one another. Somehow the sad thought for Ms. Carrie brought the good memories of the love they knew she had for them. Her kind, calm, and loving ways. She seemed to know just when a gentle hug was needed. Even when she didn't recognize them, she had a kind and pleasant smile on her face.

Michelle and Daniel knew one of Ms. Carrie's favorite church songs was "Count Your Blessings." They realized how blessed they were to be Ms. Carrie's great-grandchildren.

God bless Ms. Carrie.

About the Author

Having recently retired, writing this story had been a long-awaited labor of love. Carolyn Williams' mother had many outrages and comical things to say during her dementia. Between her utterances and the many dreams Carolyn has, she hopes to tell more stories. Her problem is procrastination. She will stop putting things off someday.

CPSIA information can be obtained
at www.ICGtesting.com
Printed in the USA
BVHW021433290321
603654BV00013B/834

9 781098 080525